The Wheels on the Bus

and

The Boat on the Waves

Retold by Wes Magee
Illustrated by Richard Morgan

Crabtree Publishing Company

www.crabtreebooks.com

Crabtree Publishing Company
www.crabtreebooks.com
1-800-387-7650

PMB 59051, 350 Fifth Ave.
59th Floor,
New York, NY 10118

616 Welland Ave.
St. Catharines, ON
L2M 5V6

Published by Crabtree Publishing in 2013
Printed in Hong Kong/012013/BK20121102

Series editor: Melanie Palmer
Editor: Kathy Middleton
Proofreader: Crystal Sikkens
Series advisors: Dr. Hilary Minns, Catherine Glavina
Series designer: Peter Scoulding
Production coordinator and
  Prepress technician: Margaret Amy Salter
Print coordinator: Katherine Berti

All rights reserved. No part
of this publication may be
reproduced, stored in a retrieval
system, or transmitted in any
form or by any means, electronic,
mechanical, photocopy, recording
or otherwise, without the prior
written permission of the
copyright owner.

The rights of Wes Magee to be
identified as the author of The
Boat on the Waves and Richard
Morgan as the illustrator of this
Work have been asserted.

First published in 2010
by Franklin Watts
(A division of Hachette
Children's Books)

Text (The Boat on the Waves)
© Wes Magee 2010
Illustration © Richard Morgan 2010

Library and Archives Canada
Cataloguing in Publication

Magee, Wes, 1939-
    The wheels on the bus ; and, The boat on
the waves / retold by Wes Magee ; illustrated by
Richard Morgan.

(Tadpoles: nursery rhymes)
Issued also in electronic format.
ISBN 978-0-7787-1148-3 (bound).--ISBN 978-0-
7787-1152-0 (pbk.)

    1. Nursery rhymes, English. I. Morgan,
Richard, 1942- II. Title. III. Title: Boat on the
waves. IV. Series: Tadpoles (St. Catharines, Ont.).
Nursery rhymes

PZ8.3.M34Wh 2013   j398.8   C2012-907346-6

Library of Congress
Cataloging-in-Publication Data

Magee, Wes, 1939-
  [Poetry. Selections]
  The wheels on the bus ; and The boat on the waves
/ retold by Wes Magee ; illustrated by Richard
Morgan.
      pages cm. -- (Tadpoles: nursery rhymes)
  Summary: Presents the traditional nursery rhyme,
a line at a time then as a whole, followed by a new
rhyme. Includes "Notes for adults" and reading tips.
  ISBN 978-0-7787-1148-3 (reinforced library binding
: alk. paper) -- ISBN 978-0-7787-1152-0 (pbk. : alk.
paper) -- ISBN 978-1-4271-9308-7 (electronic pdf) --
ISBN 978-1-4271-9232-5 (electronic html)
1. Nursery rhymes. 2. Children's poetry. [1.
Nursery rhymes.] I. Morgan, Richard, 1942-
illustrator. II. Magee, Wes, 1939- Wheels on the bus
III. Magee, Wes, 1939- Boat on the waves IV. Title.

  PZ8.3.M2685Wh 2013
  398.8--dc23
                                    2012043748

The Wheels on the Bus

Richard Morgan

"I thought it'd be fun to draw a bus in a tropical setting, with all the unusual animals that live there. Which ones can you spot?"

The wheels
on the bus go
round and round,

round and round,
round and round.

7

The wheels on
the bus go

round and round,

9

all through the town.

11

The Wheels on the Bus

The wheels on the bus go

round and round,

round and round,

round and round.

The wheels on the bus go

round and round,

all through the town.

Can you point to the repeated words?

The Boat on the Waves

by Wes Magee
Illustrated by Richard Morgan

Wes Magee

"It's exciting to go on a boat trip across the sea. But watch out, the waves going up and down can make you seasick!"

The boat on the waves
goes up and down,

up and down,
up and down.

17

The boat on the
waves goes
up and down.

Splish! Splash! Splosh!

The Boat on the Waves

The boat on the waves

goes up and down,

 up and down,

up and down.

The boat on the waves

goes up and down.

Splish! Splash! Splosh!

 Can you point to the
repeated words?

Puzzle Time!

How many boats can you see in this picture?

Notes for adults

TADPOLES NURSERY RHYMES are structured for emergent readers.
The books may also be used for read-alouds or shared reading with young children.

The language of nursery rhymes is often already familiar to an emergent reader. Seeing the rhymes in print helps build phonemic awareness skills. The alternative rhymes extend and enhance the reading experience further, and encourage children to be creative with language and make up their own rhymes.

IF YOU ARE READING THIS BOOK WITH A CHILD, HERE ARE A FEW SUGGESTIONS:

1. Make reading fun! Choose a time to read when you and the child are relaxed and have time to share the story.
2. Recite the nursery rhyme together before you start reading. What might the alternative rhyme be about? Brainstorm ideas.
3. Encourage the child to reread the rhyme and to retell it using his or her own words. Invite the child to use the illustrations as a guide.
4. Help the child identify the rhyming words when the whole rhymes are repeated on pages 12 and 22. This activity builds phonological awareness and decoding skills. Encourage the child to make up alternative rhymes.
5. Give praise! Children learn best in a positive environment.

IF YOU ENJOYED THIS BOOK, WHY NOT TRY ANOTHER TITLE FROM TADPOLES: NURSERY RHYMES?

Baa, Baa, Black Sheep and Baa, Baa, Pink Sheep	978-0-7787-7883-7 RLB	978-0-7787-7895-0 PB
Five Little Monkeys and Five Little Penguins	978-0-7787-1133-9 RLB	978-0-7787-1151-3 PB
Hey Diddle Diddle and Hey Diddle Doodle	978-0-7787-7884-4 RLB	978-0-7787-7896-7 PB
Humpty Dumpty and Humpty Dumpty at Sea	978-0-7787-7885-1 RLB	978-0-7787-7897-4 PB
Itsy Bitsy Spider and Itsy Bitsy Beetle	978-0-7787-7886-8 RLB	978-0-7787-7898-1 PB
Row, Row, Row Your Boat and *Ride, Ride, Ride Your Bike*	978-0-7787-1149-0 RLB	978-0-7787-1153-7 PB
Twinkle, Twinkle, Little Star and *Spaceship, Spaceship, Zooming High*	978-0-7787-1132-2 RLB	978-0-7787-1150-6 PB

VISIT WWW.CRABTREEBOOKS.COM FOR OTHER CRABTREE BOOKS.

Answers

There are seven boats in this picture.